To Mam, Dad, Steven and Daniel

First impression: 2016
© Text copyright Mark Williams
© Illustration copyright Stuart Trotter

© Rockpool Children's Books Ltd. 2016

The publisher acknowledges the support of the Welsh Books Council

ISBN: 978 1 78461 364 8

Published and printed in Wales
on paper from well managed forests by

Y Lolfa Cyf., Talybont, Ceredigion SY24 5HE
e-mail ylolfa@ylolfa.com
website www.ylolfa.com
tel 01970 832 304
fax 832 782

rockpool
children's books

Rockpool Children's Books, 15 North Street,
Marton, Warwickshire CV23 9RJ

Mark Williams

The little
Welsh Football
fan

y Lolfa

The little Welsh
football fan
was very excited...
...His mum and dad
had allowed
him to stay up late
to watch his favourite team...

...Wales!

It was exciting
...thrilling...
nerve-racking...
nail-bitingly
exciting!

7

Then Wales
scored and
they won...
and they had
qualified!

9

And what
made it doubly
exciting was... that
Mum and Dad
had promised to take
the little football
fan to the game
to watch Wales play
abroad!

That night, in bed, he dreamed
that he played for Wales.
It was a bit muddled up.

13

He scored a
penalty
against Italy...

...he scored
a screamer against
Germany...

...and a header
against
England!

The other teams
couldn't get anywhere near him!
He was Man of the Match
in every game!

16

In the months before
their trip
he read about the country
they were going to.

He learned a few words
of the language.

The day came to fly to the game.
At the airport, there
were lots of Welsh football fans...
and they all sang
'Hen Wlad Fy Nhadau'.

The aeroplane flew
over the sea,
over strange lands,
over cities!

The day before the game, they wandered around the foreign, exciting city.

There were football banners hanging from the buildings.

The day of the game came.
They joined thousands of
football fans
on their way to stadium.
He got to use the language
he'd learned while buying
a programme!

The ref blew his whistle
and the game began...
"Come on Wales!"
shouted the
little Welsh football fan...
and his mum and dad!

It was a great game.
Wales scored twice and
won the match!

The little
WELSH FOOTBALL
fan

WALES

The little
WELSH FOOTBALL
fan

*Card*FACT

Wales
played its first
competitive match on
25 March 1876 against
Scotland in Glasgow,
making it the third
oldest international
team in the world!

WALES

The Little Welsh Football Fan is just one of a whole range of publications from Y Lolfa. For a full list of books currently in print, send now for your free copy of our new full-colour catalogue. Or simply surf into our website

www.ylolfa.com

for secure on-line ordering.

TALYBONT CEREDIGION CYMRU SY24 5HE
e-mail ylolfa@ylolfa.com
website www.ylolfa.com
phone (01970) 832 304
fax 832 782